For Hannah, Sophie and Quibus of course

First published in the United States and Canada in 2011 by Lemniscaat USA LLC • New York
Distributed in the United States by Lemniscaat USA LLC • New York

Library of Congress Cataloging-in-Publication Data is available.
ISBN 13: 978-1-935954-00-2 (Hardcover)
Printing and binding: Worzalla, Stevens Point, WI USA
Second U.S. edition

Ingrid & Dieter Schubert

The
Umbrella

Lemniscaat

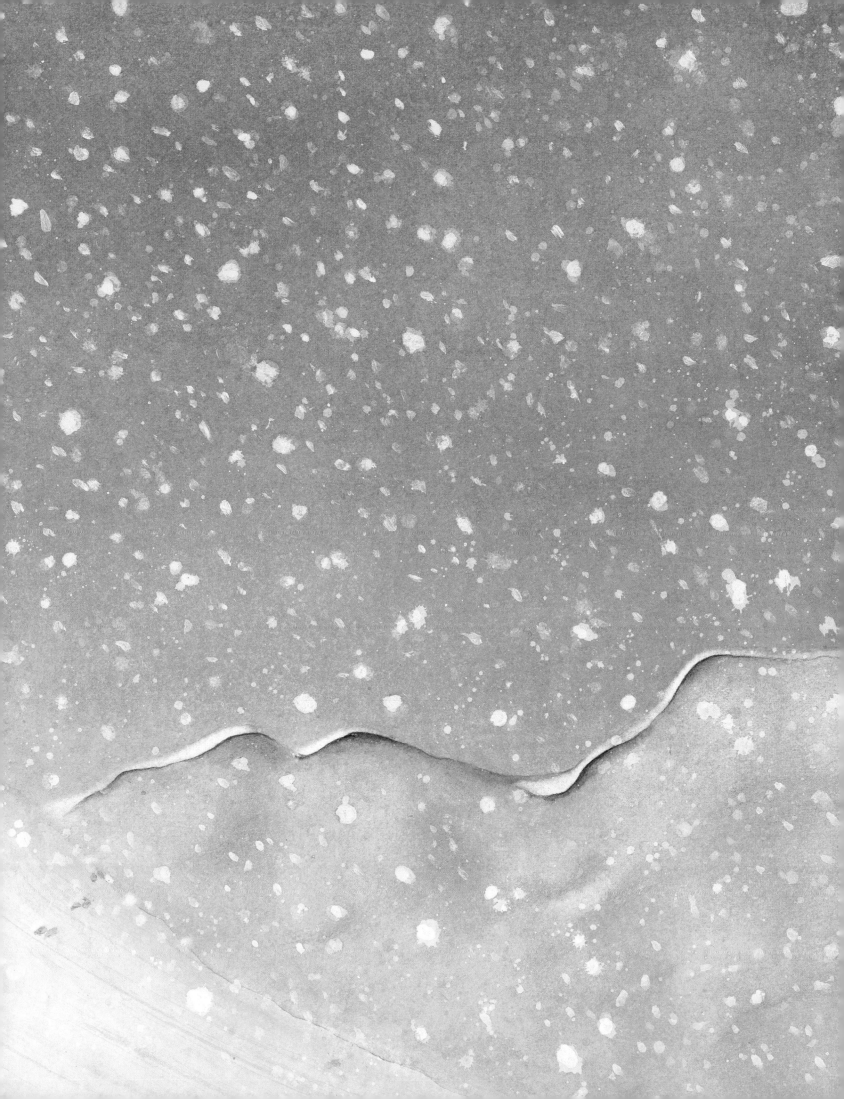